Hillary
& the Pink Tutu

Written by C. DeLayne Duffy

Illustrated by T. Michelle Durham

Hillary the Hippo and the Pink Tutu

Published by Gatekeeper Press

2167 Stringtown Rd, Suite 109

Columbus, OH 43123-2989

www.GatekeeperPress.com

Library of Congress Control Number: 2020942466

ISBN (hardcover): 9781662902239

ISBN (paperback): 9781662902222

eISBN: 9781662902215

One day Hillary went for a walk. She was very unhappy. No one knew what was wrong with her – not even Hillary. Hillary walked day and night trying to find her happiness.

As she walked by the lake, Freddy the Frog hopped up to her. 'What's wrong, Hillary?' Freddy asked.

'Oh, Freddy,' Hillary replied with tears in her eyes. 'I have lost my happiness and I don't know where to find it. I have looked everywhere!'

'Do what I do when I misplace my happiness. I hop and hop – I hop so high that my happiness always comes back.' Freddy said.

Hillary thought about it and decided she would try anything to get her happiness back.

So Hillary hopped and hopped all around the lake until she could hop no more – but still no happiness. Soon she came to some trees where she saw Shelly the Sparrow.

'What's wrong, Hillary?' Shelly asked.

'I have lost my happiness and I don't know where to find it. I have looked everywhere,' Hillary said.

"Do what I do when I have misplaced my happiness. I fly!" The words no sooner left her mouth when she spread her wings and soared up towards the clouds and over the treetops.

Hillary watched as her friend flew away. *I will try anything to get my happiness back,* Hillary thought.

Hillary raised her arms and began to flap – she flapped and flapped until she could flap no more. She jumped off rocks and the tallest hills, but she could not soar like her friend. She flapped so much that she thought her arms might fall off! *Would she ever find her happiness?*

Hillary continued to walk and walk until she came across Sammy the Squirrel picking up nuts and storing them for the winter. "What's wrong, Hillary?" Sammy asked.

'Oh, Sammy! I have lost my happiness and I don't know where to find it. I have looked everywhere!' Hillary cried.

'Do what I do when I have misplaced my happiness. I climb and climb the tallest trees!' Sammy yelled as he scampered up the nearest tree.

Hillary watched her friend as he climbed through the thick branches. She stared at the tree and thought. *I am not sure about climbing trees but if it worked for Sammy, I am sure it will work for me.*

So Hillary went and found the tallest tree, and she climbed and climbed until she could climb no more. But still no happiness.

She continued to walk and walk until she came across Charlie the Cheetah lying in the tall grass.

'What's wrong, Hillary?' Charlie asked, yawning.

'Oh, Charlie! I have lost my happiness and I don't know where to find it. I have looked everywhere,' Hillary said.

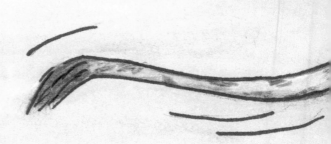

Charlie sat up and stretched. 'Do what I do when I have misplaced my happiness. I run and run as fast as I can!' As the words came out of Charlie's mouth, he ran off as fast as he could.

Hillary watched her friend disappear over the green hills. Hillary thought, *Well, if running works for Charlie, it will surely work for me!*

Hillary ran and ran until she could run no more – but still no happiness. By now, Hillary was even unhappier than she was before. It seemed hopeless! If all of her friends could find their happiness – why couldn't she? After all, she did everything her friends did to find their happiness. As she made her way through the tall grass, past the trees, and around the lake, Hillary came across a sight she had never seen before.

There in the clearing – twirling and spinning
– was Rachel the Rabbit. Hillary was truly
amazed. She had never seen a more graceful
and beautiful sight. She walked up to Rachel
and asked, 'What are you doing, Rachel?'

"I'm dancing! I dance when I lose my happiness!" Rachel said as she continued to twirl in circles. Hillary watched her friend spin this way and that way. "Do you think I could do that? Can I twirl and spin just like you?" Hillary asked with wide eyes.

Rachel stopped twirling and looked at her friend. 'Of course you can! Anyone can if you can hear the music!' Hillary had her doubts. Rachel sensed her friend's hesitation. 'I have an idea!' she said as she raced

towards home. She returned, handing Hillary the pinkest and frilliest tutu. 'If you wear this you can dance like you have never danced before!' Hillary put on the tutu – a strange feeling came over her and she started twirling and spinning. She twirled this way, and she twirled that way. She spun fast, and she spun slow.

Freddy the Frog, Sammy the Squirrel, Shelly the Sparrow, and Charlie the Cheetah walked through the clearing and saw Rachel and Hillary dancing and laughing.

Shelly said, 'I guess Hillary found her
happiness at last.' They were happy for
their friend. They sat down and watched
as the odd pair continued to dance and
prance around.

The one thing Hilary did not realize was that she had her happiness all along. It was never lost. She could not depend on others to make her happy. She had to search deep inside herself and find her own music. The music of contentment, happiness and – of course – DANCE!

This is where happiness comes from – YOURSELF!

Be content in yourself...

Be happy with yourself....

Keep YOUR music alive!

Made in the USA
Coppell, TX
18 October 2022

84886336R00017